# sometimes I PRETEND

by Kirk Roberts

illustrated by Jeannie Winston

To Boe and Graham.

*A Discovery Toys Book*

Published by Discovery Toys, Pleasant Hill, California
Printed in Singapore  Designed by Yvonne Smith

**S**ometimes I have to
do things I don't like...
so sometimes I pretend.

Sometimes when

...have to go to bed...

I pretend I'm taking

off in a spaceship.

Sometimes when

...have to take a bath...

I pretend I'm i

jungle pond.

Sometimes when I have

o clean up my room...

I pretend I'm discov

...ing buried treasure.

Sometimes when I have

to pick up my laundry...

I pretend I'm feeding

a friendly dolphin.

Sometimes when I he

e to walk a long way...

I pretend I'm a giant wall

...g across the countryside.

Sometimes when

...have to share my toys...

I pretend I'r

Santa Claus.

Sometimes when I have to

stay inside on a rainy day...

I pretend I'm swin

...ning in a fish bowl.

**S**ometimes when I have to s

...y in the car for a long time...

I pretend I'm riding

n a roller coaster.

Sometimes when I have

...to clean up my spilt milk...

I pretend that I'v

stopped a flood.

get a shot from the doctor...

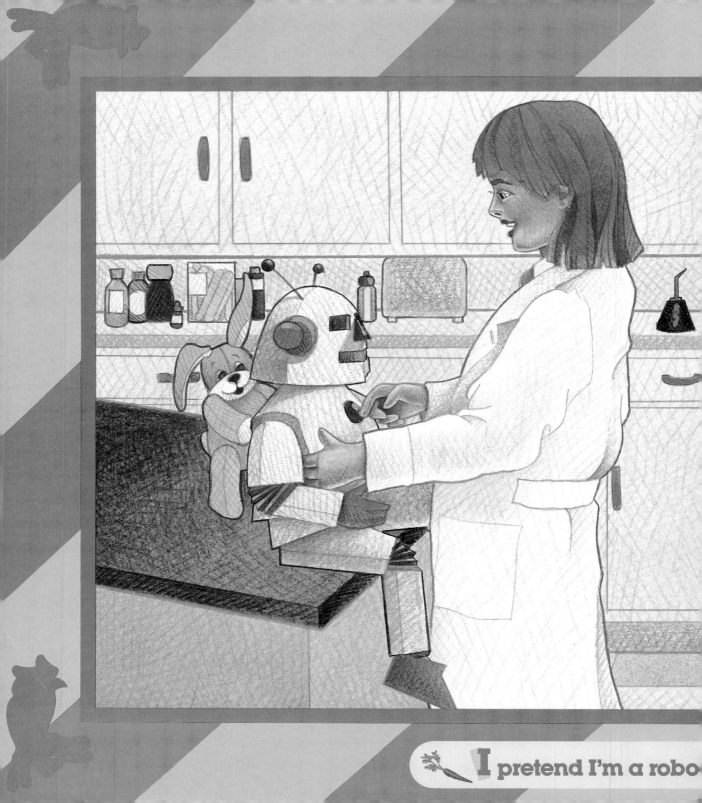

I pretend I'm a robo

And it doesn't even hurt.

Sometimes when I am asked to eat m

vegetables, I pretend I'm not hungry...

But tonight I don't have to pret

d! Because we're having pizza!